ELIZABETH JENNINGS was born in Lincolnshire in 1926, and has spent most of her life in Oxford. Having had many volumes of poetry published, Elizabeth has become a classic in her own time, winning awards as diverse as the Somerset Maugham Award and the W.H. Smith Literary Award. She is one of our most accessible and best-loved poets of today.

Elizabeth Jennings

A Spell of Words

Selected Poems *for* Children

MACMILLAN

First published 1997 by Macmillan Children's Books

This edition published 1998 by Macmillan Children's Books
a division of Macmillan Publishers Limited
25 Eccleston Place, London SW1W 9NF
and Basingstoke

Associated companies throughout the world

ISBN 330 35422 1

5 7 9 8 6 4

A CIP catalogue record for this book is available from the British Library.

Phototypeset by Intype London Ltd

Printed by Mackays of Chatham plc, Kent

The publisher and author are indebted to Anne Harvey and Roger Pringle for their assistance in the production of this book.

For John Gielgud

Contents

After the Ark

The First Music

Emerging from a Cloud

Waking, I Find Myself Alone

Our World Dreams Deep

Introduction

When Elizabeth Jennings was a small girl she thought, "How wonderful it would be to write a poem" but believed it to be a talent she would never possess. It was later, aged 13, that she was inspired by hearing G.K. Chesterton's poem *Lepanto*, and then wrote a poem herself.

"It was a very bad poem," she says, but she was excited by its shape and rhythm . . . and, "I was delighted that I could rhyme and scan." Like many young writers she strived too hard for effect in her early poems – they were over-dramatic and derivative – so it was a wise adult who guided her in the right direction by praising her smallest, simplest effort – a mere four lines – about a dead bird:

> I held it in my hand
>   With its little hanging head.
> It was soft and light and whole,
>   But it was dead.

In her book *Let's Have Some Poetry*, she wrote, "This, then, was a poem which arose entirely out of my own experience. I had held the dead bird in my own hand and it had provoked in me a curious mixture of feelings, feelings which only came clear for me, as it were, when I wrote this four-line poem. For one of the most extraordinary things about writing poetry is that it clarifies, and indeed reveals, what one has thought and felt."

If that is so for the poet it is equally true for the

reader, and one of Elizabeth Jennings' special qualities is the way she evokes feelings and incidents that we recognise, but could not put into words so memorably. When she recalls, for instance, the child she once was, frightened at night, curious, unsure, lonely at school:

> Legs in knee-socks
> Standing on the rough playground
> Suddenly thinking, "Why am I here?"

As a young writer herself she took seriously T.S. Eliot's remark that "a young poet hasn't anything to say" and that what was important was "craftsmanship not content". She considers now that her long apprenticeship with the tools of poetry gave her something to write when she eventually "found something worth writing about". That "something" has ranged widely across her gregarious interests in people, life, the arts, and this *Selected Poems for Children* has been worth waiting for. The readers will undoubtedly be "children of all ages": the poems perhaps originally conceived with the younger reader in mind are entirely ageless, and many of her "adult" poems will speak lucidly to the young.

Twelve years ago I wrote of Elizabeth Jennings that, through reading her poetry, I was persuaded to look with a fresh eye at myself. The same is true today. She retains the ability to understate or startle in a line and once said: "Writing poetry seemed to be another way of finding out what life and the world meant."

Anne Harvey
1996

A Golden Key

A Classroom

The day was wide and that whole room was wide,
The sun slanting across the desks, the dust
Of chalk rising. I was listening
As if for the first time,
As if I'd never heard our tongue before,
As if a music came alive for me.
And so it did upon the lift of language,
A battle poem, *Lepanto*. In my blood
The high call stirred and brimmed.
I was possessed yet coming for the first
Time into my own
Country of green and sunlight,
Place of harvest and waiting
Where the corn would never all be garnered but
Leave in the sun always at least one swathe.
So from a battle I learnt this healing peace,
Language a spell over the hungry dreams,
A password and a key. That day is still
Locked in my mind. When poetry is spoken
That door is opened and the light is shed,
The gold of language tongued and minted fresh.
And later I began to use my words,
Stared into verse within that classroom and
Was called at last only by kind inquiry
"How old are you?" "Thirteen"
"You are a thinker". More than thought it was
That caught me up excited, charged and changed,
Made ready for the next fine spell of words,
Locked into language with a golden key.

Star-Gazing

Give it a name. It is still there,
One on its own, another star
   Which is not yours and is not mine.

And yet we need to find a name,
To lay indeed a kind of claim,
   A beauty wrought to our design.

But we are wrong. We don't possess
The stars. Our words make them grow less
   As we waylay them to define.

They shine a love. Another one
Is there tonight. The Summer sun
   Left the horizon's steady line.

Think, there are more than we can count,
Star after star, O such amount,
   Each seems to flicker out a sign,

To hand a message. It is this:
"We are much further than you guess
   And brighter too. Yes, we combine

Distance and light to give a show
Like fireworks which retain their glow,
   We keep a rich unmeasured shine."

The voices pause. I look again,
The sky is pouring silver rain
   Which could be yours and might be mine.

A Sort of Chinese Poem

The Chinese write poems
That don't look like poems.
They are more like paintings.

A cherry-tree, a snow-storm,
An old man in a boat –
These might be their subjects.

It all looks so easy –
But it isn't.
You have to be very simple,
Very straightforward,
To see so clearly.
Also, you have to have thousands of years of skill.

When I was a child, I once wrote a Chinese poem.
Now I'm too complicated.

A Performance of Henry V at Stratford-upon-Avon

Nature teaches us our tongue again
And the swift sentences came pat. I came
Into cool night rescued from rainy dawn.
And I seethed with language – Henry at
Harfleur and Agincourt came apt for war
In Ireland and the Middle East. Here was
The riddling and right tongue, the feeling words
Solid and dutiful. Aspiring hope
Met purpose in "advantages" and "He
That fights with me today shall be my brother."
Say this is patriotic, out of date.
But you are wrong. It never is too late

For nights of stars and feet that move to an
Iambic measure; all who clapped were linked,
The theatre is our treasury and too,
Our study, school-room, house where mercy is

Dispensed with justice. Shakespeare has the mood
And draws the music from the dullest heart.
This is our birthright, speeches for the dumb
And unaccomplished. Henry has the words
For grief and we learn how to tell of death
With dignity. "All was as cold" she said
"As any stone" and so, we who lacked scope
For big or little deaths, increase, grow up
To purposes and means to face events
Of cruelty, stupidity. I walked

Fast under stars. The Avon wandered on
"Tomorrow and tomorrow". Words aren't worn
Out in this place but can renew our tongue,
Flesh out our feeling, make us apt for life.

Ballad of War

Brutal and vigilant the watchers were,
Pale and lean and disciplined to hate.
They taught us fear because they knew white fear
So well. They stood as sentries at the gate.

Gate of the morning and the dawn's endeavour,
Gate of the mind with fantasies and war,
Gate of sickness and unconquered fever,
Yet haven't we known all such gates before?

The gate of birth and then the broken cord,
The gate of love and holding back from fear,
The gate of language and the golden word
Which speaking makes the lustre disappear?

Who are the watchers? Why won't you reply?
Is the world sick? You turn away in dread.
What are those shadows widening the sky?
Where are the stars and is the new moon dead?

Think Of

Think of a note
And a drop of water
Falls and splashes and
See the taut blue
And a cloud cruising, a
Golden shaft of
Riches and
Then comes a theme,
An easy drift,
A pluck on a harp, a
Call on a horn
And then see
In the mind's eye
In the heart's ear
In the reaching hand
And the beat of a heart
To a somewhere coming
Choir of angels
Where seraphs blow
A trumpet of sound
And a colour enters
Imagination's
Ajar door
And we are aware
Of a threshold crossed
Of a shadow woven
In webs of air
And more of all
Always more and more

An Attempt to Charm Sleep

A certain blue
A very dark one
Navy-blue
Going to school
Get back to colour
A pale blue
Somebody's eyes
Or were they grey
Who was the person
Did they like me
Go back to colour
An intolerant blue
A very deep
Inviting water
Is it a river
Where is it going
Shall I swim
What is its name
Go back to colour
Go back to waking
The spell doesn't work
As I stare at the night
It seems like blue.

Casting a Spell

Learn a spell. It takes some time
First you must have the gift of rhyme,
New images, a melody.
Verse will do but poetry
Sometimes will come if you have luck.
Play tunes, blow trumpets, learn to pluck
The harp. The best of spells are cast
When you have written words to last,
Rich in subtle rhythms and
Right words which most will understand.
Casting a spell's a secret skill
Which few learn fast. No act of will
On your part hands the gift to you.
Words must surprise and yet ring true.
False sorcerers are everywhere
But the true magic's deep and rare.

In Praise of Creation

The Animals' Arrival

So they came
Grubbing, rooting, barking, sniffing,
Feeling for cold stars, for stone, for some hiding-place,
Loosed at last from heredity, able to eat
From any tree or from ground, merely mildly themselves,
And every movement was quick, was purposeful, was
  proposed.
The galaxies gazed on, drawing in their distances.
The beasts breathed out warm on the air.

No-one had come to make anything of this,
To move it, name it, shape it a symbol;
The huge creatures were their own depth, the hills
Lived lofty there, wanting no climber.
Murmur of birds came, rumble of underground beasts
And the otter swam deftly over the broad river.

There was silence too.
Plants grew in it, it wove itself, it spread, it enveloped
The evening as day-calls died and the universe hushed,
  hushed.
A last bird flew, a first beast swam
And prey on prey
Released each other
(Nobody hunted at all):
They slept for the waiting day.

Bird Study

A worm writhes and you have some power
Of knowing when and where to strike.
Then suddenly bread in a shower.
Being a bird is like

This and a feathered overcoat,
A throb of sound, a balanced wing,
A quiver of the beak and throat,
A gossip-mongering.

But higher up a hawk will take
Stature of stars, a comet-fall,
Or else a swan that oars a lake,
Or one note could be all.

I am obsessed with energy
I never touch. I am alive
To what I only hear and see,
The sweep, the sharp, the drive.

Goldfinch

These claws too contain
A bad crop. The goldfinch preys on the blossom
Of apple, that froth and tide of a white
Spring wedding. The neatness, the tailor-made
Touch of his suit bespeaks a harmlessness,
A wish to please that he is stranger to.

Why must we pet the world's destroyers?
I am not speaking of the soft-handed cream-buyers
Or the vendors of fresh liver
To fill the guts of a cat, no, I speak
A contradiction. I praise the pluck of the goldfinch
But I abhor this lamentable *gourmet*
Who plucks from the Eden branch the Eden flower,
Such a bright appearance, such a dandy to the inch.

Tiffany: a Burmese Kitten

(who is real)

For Mrs Graham Greene

My friends keep mice – white ones and patched.
I wish I could pretend
I really like the creatures, but
I cannot and I spend

Just hours and hours admiring them.
I think my friends soon guess
They're not my kind of animal.
My secret wish, oh, yes,

Is for a Burmese kitten, one
Of those pure chocolate brown
Cats that I know are seldom seen
In any usual town.

I once met one called Tiffany;
She used to come and see
Me when I was in hospital.
She'd jump all over me,

Knock flowers down, explore the place
From door to door, and leap
Up all the tawdry furniture.
I know she helped me sleep:

I know she helped me get quite well,
Although I did not see
That at the time she came she was
Doctor and nurse to me.

Hatching

His night has come to an end and now he must break
The little sky which shielded him. He taps
Once and nothing happens. He tries again
And makes a mark like lightning. He must thunder,
Storm and shake and break a universe
Too small and safe. His daring beak does this.

And now he is out in a world of smells and spaces.
He shivers. Any air is wind to him.
He huddles under wings but does not know
He is already shaping feathers for
A lunge into the sky. His solo flight
Will bring the sun upon his back. He'll bear it,
Carry it, learn the real winds, by instinct
Return for food and, larger than his mother,
Avid for air, harry her with his hunger.

Sparrow

The hallowed, the special flyer, I mean the sparrow,
A flash of feathers and tiny body, a quick
Nerve, a spirit of speed and certainly one
To copy when you are tempted to turn from the sun.
Sparrow of "special providence" teach to us
Your joy, your gladness, your success, for you
Live in accord with that power which moves
You fast and far. Your flights and pauses bring
Delight to us. We are not surprised you were chosen
Specially, for even birds who sing
With a rapture of angels lack your flare and fling.

In Praise of Creation

That one bird, one star,
The one flash of the tiger's eye
Purely assert what they are,
Without ceremony testify.

Testify to order, to rule –
How the birds mate at one time only,
How the sky is, for a certain time, full
Of birds, the moon sometimes cut thinly.

And the tiger trapped in the cage of his skin,
Watchful over creation, rests
For the blood to pound, the drums to begin,
Till the tigress' shadow casts

A darkness over him, a passion, a scent,
The world goes turning, turning, the season
Sieves earth to its one sure element
And the blood beats beyond reason.

Then quiet, and birds folding their wings,
The new moon waiting for years to be stared at here,
The season sinks to satisfied things –
Man with his mind ajar.

The Ark

Nobody knows just how they went.
They certainly went in two by two,
But who preceded the kangaroo
And who dared follow the elephant?

"I've had enough," said Mrs Noah.
"The food just won't go round," she said.
A delicate deer raised up his head
As if to say, "*I* want no more."

In they marched and some were sick.
All very well for those who could be
On the rough or the calm or the middle sea.
But I must say that ark felt very thick

Of food and breath. How wonderful
When the dove appeared and rested upon
The hand of Noah. All fear was gone,
The sea withdrew, the air was cool.

After the Ark

The Animals' Chorus

Once there was nothing but water and air. The air
Broke into constellations, waters withdrew.
The sun was born and itself hatched out first light.
Rocks appeared and sand, and on the rocks
There was movement. Under the sea
Something tender survived, not yet a fish
A nameless object floating. This was how we

Began and how you later followed us,
Much, much later, long before clocks or sun-dials,
Long before time was discovered.
The sun stared hard and the moon looked back and
   mountains
Pierced the air. Snow was formed, this earth
Was gently beginning to live.
We were your fore-runners, we with fins and tails,
With wings and legs. Under the sun we crawled
To life. How good the air was, how sweet the green
Leaves, the rock-pools, the sturdy trees. And flowers

Flaunted such fragrance we wandered among them, clung
To their petals or, out of the blue and widespread air,
Descended, drew in our wings and settled where
You now stand or sit or walk. We know
So much about you. We are your family tree
But you have power over us for you can name,
And naming is like possession. It's up to you
To give us our liberty or to make us tame.

The Fish's Warning

Stay by the water, stand on your shadow, stare
At my quick gliding, my darting body. You're made of air
And I of water. I do not know if you mean to throw
Your line, I move very fast, swim with fins much quicker
Than your thin arms. Rushes will hide me and will
Darken me. I'm a pulse of silver, something the moon
  tossed down.
I am frail for your finding but one whom only the night
  can drown.

The Ladybird's Story

It was a roadway to me;
So many meeting-places and directions.
It was smooth, polished, sometimes it shook a little
But I did not tumble off.
I heard you say, and it was like a siren,
"A ladybird. Good luck. Perhaps some money."
I did not understand.
Suddenly I was frightened, fearful of falling
Because you lifted your hand.

And then I saw your eyes,
Glassy moons always changing shape,
Sometimes suns in eclipse.
I watched the beak, the peak of your huge nose
And the island of your lips.
I was afraid but you were not. I have
No sting. I do not wound.
I carry a brittle coat. It does not protect.
I thought you would blow me away but superstition
Saved me. You held your hand now in one position,
Gentled me over the veins and arteries.
But it was not I you cared about but money.
You see I have watched you with flies.

The Cabbage White Butterfly

I look like a flower you could pick. My delicate wings
Flutter over the cabbages. I don't make
Any noise ever. I'm among silent things.
  Also I easily break.

I have seen the nets in your hands. At first I thought
A cloud had come down but then I noticed you
With your large pink hand and arm. I was nearly caught
  But fortunately I flew

Away in time, hid while you searched, then took
To the sky, was out of your reach. Like a nameless flower
I tried to appear. Can't you be happy to look?
  Must you possess with your power?

The Moth's Plea

I am a disappointment
And much worse.
You hear a flutter, you expect a brilliance of wings,
Colours dancing, a bright
Flutter, but then you see
A brown, bedraggled creature
With a shamefaced, unclean look
Darting upon your curtains and clothes,
Fighting against the light.
I hate myself. It's no wonder you hate me.

I meddle among your things,
I make a meal out of almost any cloth,
I hide in cupboards and scare
Any who catch me unaware.
I am your enemy – the moth.

You try to keep me away
But I'm wily and when I do
Manage to hide, you chase me, beat me, put
Horrible-smelling balls to poison me.
Have you ever thought what it's like to be
A parasite,
Someone who gives you a fright,
Who envies the rainbow colours of the bright
Butterflies who hover round flowers all day?

O please believe that I do understand how it feels
To be awake in and be afraid of the night.

The Spider's Confession

You with your looms and wheels and every kind of
machine,
Don't you marvel at the intricate lace I spin?
Many of you are skilful but have you seen
Working under your hands such delicacy, such thin,
Easily breakable patterns? You think it strange

That one with a squashy, dark and ugly body,
Can make such a wonder. I wish that I could convince
All of you that it hurts to carry around
A creature so greatly at odds with the work it spins.
Some of you are revolted at sight of me
And quickly wash me down drains. All that I ask is that
you
At least allow me to do
My work. That is all I honestly want you to see.

Wasp in a Room

Chase me, follow me round the room, knock over
Chairs and tables, bruise knees, spill books. High
I am then. If you climb up to me I go
Down. I have ways of detecting your least
Movements. I have radar you did not
Invent. You are afraid of me. I can
Sting hard. Ah but watch me bask in
The, to you, unbearable sun. I sport with it, am
Its jester and also its herald. Fetch a
Fly whisk. I scorn such. You must invent stings
For yourselves or else leave me alone, small, flying
Buzzing tiger who have made a jungle out of the room
 you thought safe,
Secure from all hurts and prying.

The Snake's Warning

A coil of power,
A twist of speed,
Hider in grass,
Content in jungles,
Footless, wingless,
I have powers beasts lack,
Strength birds seek
In clean skies which
Are not my home.
If footsteps approach
Or I hear a twig
Break I alert
At once. My tongue
Means painful death.
Keep your hands off me.

There are men, a few,
With a special gift
To whom I surrender.
I sway to the sound
Of their flutes but I keep
My glance upon them.
They hypnotise me,
Don't ask me how
Or when or why,
If *you* want to be safe,
Keep away, don't try
To tame me with flutes.
If you do, you will die.

The Earthworm's Monologue

Birds prey on me, fish are fond of my flesh.
My body is like a sausage, it lacks the snake's
Sinuous splendour and colour. Yes, I'm absurd.
Yet I also till and soften the soil, I prepare
The way for flowers, Spring depends upon me
At least a little. Mock me if you will,
Cut me in half, I'll come together again.
But haven't you felt a fool, hated your shape,
Wanted to hide? If so I am your friend;
I would sympathise with you were I not so busy
But bend down over me, you who are not yet tall
And be proud of all you contain in a body so small.

The Frogs' History

You caught and carried us, pleased with yourselves.
We were only blobs of black in jars.

You knew what we'd become, were glad to wait.
How hectically we swam in that glass cage!

And there was never hope of an escape.
You put us on a shelf with more care than

You generally move. We were a hope,
A something-to-look-forward to, a change,

Almost a conjuring trick. Some sleight of nature
Would, given time, change us to your possessions.

We would be green and glossy, wet to touch.
"Take them away," squeamish grown-ups would

Call out. Not you. You longed to hold us in
Your dry palms with surprising gentleness

And with a sense of unexpected justice
Would let us go, wanted to see us leap

And watch our eyes which never seem to sleep,
Hear our hideous but lively croak.

We know as well as you we are a joke.

The Bats' Plea

Ignore the stories which say
We shall fly to and tangle your hair,
That you are wise if you dread
Our mouse-like bodies, the way
Our wings fan out and spread
In gloom, in dusty air.

Eagles are lucky to be
Thought of in terms of light
And glory. Half-bird, half-beast,
We're an anomaly.
But, clinging to darkness we rest
And, like stars, belong to the night.

The Swallows' Speech

We are the bearers of sun, we take
Its rays with us, it rides our wings
And trusts its gold to us. The sky
Enlarges southward, opens for
Our passage. Watch our nestlings fly
After. We carry all warm things.

You in the Winter only know
Our arrow ways in dreams. We keep
A little glow within your minds,
We stoke your loving and your sleep.
Listen, our wings are coming back.
Summer is on. We tell you so.

Gull Thought

Shall I descend? Shall I allow
A buffet of wind to take me? Shall
I hover to stillness over the tides,
Smelling the salt, waiting to pounce
And bruise the waves? The sun's gold slides
Over my wings. I am wide awake
And the earth is mine to take.

I descend to a place of waves and hands,
To water-filled air, to spume and to
Five fingers holding me food. I am
August and insolent. Hands, wait there!
I will skim the horizon before I turn,
A tide of my own, and grasp the bread,
Following instinct, possessing the air.

The Rooks' Chorus

Our homes are high,
We sway in the sun and wind
And are not afraid
Of a stormy sky.
At night we sleep
Close to the moon and stars.
Think of us as the deep
Note of the songs which fill your mind
As a lullaby.

Early risers are we.
We want to veer
About as the sun rises
Magnificently.
We open our wings
To protect more fragile things.
Look up at us when you wake
And the turns and curves we make
And fashion your day with the songs
We sing to ease you awake.

The Robin's Song

I am cheerful. You can
Depend on me. I'm around
All the year. In the rain,
When frost is on the ground
Or the sun is dancing, I'm here,
Bright in colour and sound.

Other birds are less stout,
Sing flawless songs in Spring,
Look more beautiful, there's no doubt.
I am always pleased when you fling
Crumbs to me. Yes, I am happy.
Isn't that everything?

The Sparrows' Chorus

How often you forget about us! We are
About all through the year.
Our feathers are drab, beside other birds we appear
Nonentities, no fashion parades for us.
Nobody makes a fuss
Of us and really we don't care,
At least, not too much.
But we are faithful, whatever the weather we stay
Among you. And don't think we're ungrateful for the
 food
Some of you like to toss.
We need it badly. We can lose half our weight
On an icy night. We depend a lot on you.

Often, we have to admit, we wish we wore
Flamboyant colours. A yellow, a red, a blue.
The robin is lucky and all the tits are too.
But perhaps our smallness is noticeable. Beside
A starling or blackbird we are almost invisible
But don't forget we are here,
Domestic creatures, never flying far.
Just to exist through an English climate is
Remarkable.
It's almost a miracle simply that we are.

The Thrush Confides

The truth about me is I am
One who enjoys life, who feels
Happy most of the time.
Whatever weather may come –
Wind, rain, enormous falls
Of snow – I feel at home
And would like you to feel much the same.

And please don't imagine that I
Am stupid or priggish. I'm not.
I know I'm not handsome, not one
Who people point at and cry
"What a very remarkable sight."
I like being left alone
To find worms, look about, feel the sun.

The Owl's Request

Do not be frightened of me.
I am a night-time creature. When the earth is still,
When trees are shadows of shadows,
When only the moon and its attendant stars
Enlarge the night, when the smallest sound is shrill
And may wake you up and frighten you,
I am about with my friendly "Tu-whit, tu whoo".

My face is kindly but also mysterious.
People call me wise.
Perhaps they do so because I sometimes close my
eyes
And seem to be thinking.
The way I think is not like yours. I need
No thick philosopher's book;
I can tell the truth of the world with a look
But I do not speak about
What I see there. Think of me then
As the certainty in your wandering nights.
I can soothe men
And will snatch you out of your doubt,
Bear you away to the stars and moon
And to sleep and dawn. So lie
And listen to my lullaby.

The Cuckoo's Speech

What a very bad example I set
But never mind.
I have the best of all worlds. I get
Applause and kind
Words from all when they hear the sound
Of me. Winter's behind

And I prove Spring's arrived. Forget the way
I use the homes
Of others, set up house there, always lay
My eggs in the warm
Hard-worked-for nests. O yes, you can certainly say
To me all good luck comes.

The Lion Cub

My fur is soft. I am not a lion yet.
You can tease me a little, treat me like a pet.

The keeper is feeding my parents. Trust me to
Be playful. I can warm and comfort you.

Forget the forests and jungle, the great sun-face
Of my father. He has violence and grace

And I have neither yet. For a little time
I am a prince locked safe in a nursery rhyme.

The Cockerel Proclaims

I am proud of my pride.
I open the doors of morning.
I shout the trees awake,
Circle your towns with a high,
Magnificent, self-controlled cry.

One by one I snuff out the stars
And I am the first colours,
A reminder of the rainbow,
A singer shaming your small
Complaining voices. I'm tall

And proud of my flaring height.
I am the sun's true herald.
I wind up the small birds' voices.
And tell you it's worth getting up
As I lock the doors of the night.

The Fieldmouse's Monologue

Didn't you know how frightened I was when I came
For shelter in your room? I am not tame.
You looked enormous when I saw you first.
I rushed to the hole I had made, took refuge there,
Crouched behind paper you thrust at me, shivered with
  fear.
I had smelt some chocolate. The kitchen was warm below
And outside there was frost and, one whole night, great
  snow.

I only guessed you were frightened too when you
Called out loudly, deafeningly to me.
My ears are small but my hearing strong, you see.
You pushed old papers against my hole and so
I had to climb into a drawer. You did not know
That I could run so high. I felt your hand,
Like my world in shadow, shudder across me and
I scuttled away but felt a kind of bond
With you in your huge fear.
Was I the only friend near?

The Hedgehog's Explanation

I move very slowly,
I would like to be friendly,
Yet my prickly back has a look of danger. You might
Suppose I were ready for war or at least a fight
With a cat on the wall, a gather of birds, but no,
My prickles damage nobody, so you

Must be gentle with me, you with your huge shadow,
Your footsteps like claps of thunder.
The terrible touch of your hands.
Listen to me: I am a ball of fear,
Terror is what I know best,
What I live with and dream about.
Put out a saucer of milk for me,
Keep me from roads and cars.
If you want to look after someone.
Take care of me
And give me at least the pretence I am safe and free.

The Rabbit's Advice

I have been away too long.
Some of you think I am only a nursery tale,
One which you've grown out of.
Or perhaps you saw a movie and laughed at my ears
But rather envied my carrot.
I must tell you that I exist.

I'm a puff of wool leaping across a field,
Quick to all noises,
Smelling my burrow of safety.
I am easily frightened. A bird
Is tame compared to me.
Perhaps you have seen my fat white cousin who sits,
Constantly twitching his nose,
Behind bars in a hutch at the end of a garden.
If not, imagine those nights when you lie awake
Afraid to turn over, afraid
Of night and dawn and sleep.
Terror is what I am made
Of partly, partly of speed.

But I am a figure of fun.
I have no dignity
Which means I am never free.
So, when you are frightened or being teased, think of
My twitching whiskers, my absurd white puff of a tail,
Of all that I mean by "me"
And my ludicrous craving for love.

The Sheep's Confession

I look stupid, much like a dirty heap of snow
The Winter left.
I have nothing to draw your attention, nothing for show,
Except the craft

Which shears me and leaves me looking even more
Unintelligent.
I do not wonder you laugh when you see my bare
Flesh like a tent

Whose guy-ropes broke. But listen, I have one thing
To charm and delight –
The lamb I drop when Winter is turning to Spring.
His coat is white,

Purer than mine and he wears socks of black wool.
He can move
And prance. I am proud of a son so beautiful
And so worthy of love.

The Deers' Request

We are the disappearers.
You may never see us, never,
But if you make your way through a forest
Stepping lightly and gently,
Not plucking or touching or hurting,
You may one day see a shadow
And after the shadow a patch
Of speckled fawn, a glint
Of a horn.
  Those signs mean us.

O chase us never. Don't hurt us.
We who are male carry antlers
Horny, tough, like trees,
But we are terrified creatures,
Are quick to move, are nervous
Of the flutter of birds, of the quietest
Footfall, are frightened of every noise.

If you would learn to be gentle,
To be quiet and happy alone,
Think of our lives in deep forests,
Of those who hunt us and haunt us
And drive us into the ocean.
If you love to play by yourself
Content in that liberty,
Think of us being hunted,
Tell those men to let us be.

The Riding School

We are at grass now and the emerald meadow
Highlights our polished coats. All afternoon
You trotted, cantered us. How mild we were,
Our bodies were at one
With yours. Now we are cropping at the shadow
We throw. We scarcely stir.

You never saw us wild or being broken
In. We tossed our saddles off and ran
With streaming manes. Like Pegasus almost
We scorned the air. A man
Took long to tame us. Let your words be spoken
Gently. You own the freedom we have lost.

The Black Cat's Conversation

Do not suppose
Because I keep to the fire,
Am out half the night,
Sleep where I fall,
Eye you with stares
Like your finest marbles,
That I am not conscious
Of your slightest changes
In mood. I never
Miss your temper
Although you attempt
To disguise it. I know

How envious you are
Of my lithe body,
My lack of self-consciousness,
My glossy coat,
My imperious air.
All this is instinct,
Something you've lost
Except when you cower
From the rats I bring in,
Proud of my haul.
I am proud of my pride
And I always win.

Finale For The Animals

Some with cruelty came, sharp-fanged and clawed,
Tore at the air searching for food which, found,
They ate in an instant – new leaves, the tall and small
Flowers. Carnivores were
Worse, hunters of blood, smellers of victims
More miles away than our instruments measure or we
Imagine. Meanwhile the jungle listened and looked.
The parrot kept its beak shut, the slithering snake
Stilled to a coil. The stars were listening, the sun's
Burning paused at the tear and rampage of
A striped or spotted creature. This was the time
Before we were.

Now we have caged and enclosed but not enchanted
Most of these. Now full of power we are not
Gentle with flowers, pull too hard, break the admired
Rose with abandonment. We should know better.

You have heard of the ark and Noah. Most likely it
Was a local event or a myth but remember men
Bow down to the myths they create.
Perhaps we were kindest, most gentle,
Most at our best
When we coupled all creatures and launched them forth
  in an ark.
Imagination was gracious then indeed,
Gracious too when we thought up the speeding dove,
Feathery emblem of peace whiter than clouds, its wings
Combing and calming the breakers. The waters stilled.

You have heard now of some of these, learnt of their
  habits.
Do not haunt zoos too often, do not demand
Affection too often from rabbits or cats or dogs,
Do not tame if taming hurts.
Be grateful for such variety of manners,
For the diverse universe.
Above all respect the smallest of all these creatures
As you are awed by the stars.

The First Music

Remember

Remember wings when you think of spells,
Wings of the butterfly, wings of a swift,
Think of the sky and the loop and lift
Of the seagulls' wings and their swoop and drift.
A spell is how a bird feels

When it takes to the cloud-puffed air
And feels the wind for the first time over its wings,
Feels their delicate flutterings.
Spells are this and other things,
Often clasped in a rhyme.

When you think of spells remember the best
Dreams you had on a day of sun
When the colour of Poppy and Buttercup ran,
When the world of creatures first began
And everything was blessed.

You cannot expect or search for a spell.
It comes to you with the rise of a breeze,
Runs through your veins as wind uses trees.
It is the voice of the changing seas
Caught in the shape of a shell.

Losing and Finding

You had been searching quietly through the house
That late afternoon, Easter Saturday,
And a good day to be out of doors. But no,
I was reading in a north room. You knocked
On my door once only, despite the dark green notice,
"Do not disturb". I went at once and found you,

Paler than usual, not smiling. You just said
"I've lost them". That went a long way back
To running, screaming through a shop and knocking
Against giants. "I haven't had lunch," you said.
I hadn't much food and the shop was closed for Easter
But I found two apples and washed them both for you.

Then we went across the road, not hand in hand.
I was wary of that. You might have hated it
And anyway you were talking and I told you
About the river not far off, how some people
Swam there on a day like this. And how good the grass
Smelt as we walked to the Recreation Ground.

You were lively now as I spun you lying flat,
Talking fast when I pushed you on the swing,
Bold on the chute but obedient when, to your question
About walking up without hands, I said "Don't. You'll fall."
I kept thinking of your being lost, not crying,
But the sense of loss ran through me all the time

You were chatting away. I wanted to keep you safe,
Not know fear, be curious, love people
As you showed me when you jumped on my lap one
  evening,
Hugged me and kissed me hard. I could not keep you
Like that, contained in your joy, showing your need
As I wished *I* could. There was something elegiac

Simply because this whole thing was direct,
Chance, too, that you had found me when your parents
So strangely disappeared. There was enchantment
In the emptiness of that playground so you could
Be free for two hours only, noted by me, not you.
An Easter Saturday almost gone astray

Because you were lost and only six years old.
And it was you who rescued me, you know.
Among the swings, the meadow and the river,
You took me out of time, rubbed off on me
What it feels like to care without restriction,
To trust and never think of a betrayal.

Beginning

It is to be found half-way between sleep and waking –
A starting point, a recognition, beginning.
Think of the clouds on this planet lifted away
And the stars snapped off and the day tremendously
  breaking
And everything clear and absolute, the good morning
Striking the note of the day.

So it was and so it is always and still
Whether you notice or not. Forget that you are
Eyes, nose, ears but attend. So much must go on
Daily and hourly. Wait for the morning to fill
With cockcrow and petals unfolding, the round planet's
  power
Held in the hands of the sun.

And somewhere around are presences, always have been
Whose hands remove clouds, whose fingers prise open
  the sun.
Watch, learn the craft of beginning and seeing the world
Disclose itself. Take this down to a small thing, a keen
Whisper of wind, the sound of the cock or your own
Story that waits to be told.

I stood at a window once. I was four or five
And I watched the sun open the garden and spread out
 the grass
And heard the far choir of some blackbirds and watched
 blue flowers rise.
This was the first day for me, the planet alive
And I watched the stars' shadows grow faint and finally
 pass
And I could not believe my eyes.

Beech

They will not go. These leaves insist on staying.
Coinage like theirs looked frail six weeks ago.
What hintings at, excitement of delaying,
Almost as if some richer fruits could grow

If leaves hung on against each swipe of storm,
If branches bent but still did not give way.
Today is brushed with sun. The leaves are warm.
I picked one from the pavement and it lay

With borrowed shining on my Winter hand.
Persistence of this nature sends the pulse
Beating more rapidly. When will it end,

That pride of leaves? When will the branches be
Utterly bare, and seem like something else,
Now half-forgotten, no part of a tree?

Clouds

Have you watched the clouds this year?
Have you noticed the many changes, the diverse colours,
 the drift
And dance and jump and falling away? Have you seen
The gallant scarlet, the gentle pink, the sky
Black and purple and almost green and always
Turning inside out,
Turning and twisting and writhing and seldom still?
But when it is a glory, a feast galore,
It is like the rolling over of foam on the shore,
It is like a mountain-range, the Alps, maybe,
It is what you want to see
And what you never imagined could be, it is
A glamour, a glory of air, such bold sunsets,
Such risings up in the East. A folding of clouds
Is kind to the eyes, is a painted lullaby.
And there are few words to say why
Colours and ruffs and bubbles and bold balloons
Take our hearts, lift our spirits and glow
In our faster-beating hearts, in our minds also.
We need new words for the sky.

Fire

It is a wild animal,
It is curling round objects,
It is greasy with candles,
And they run trickling down the walls
Making tributaries.
It is as if bad weather were perpetual.

And we found it
Only just in time.
We threw wet rags on the flames
Flung the books out,
Stamped on the sparks.
At last it was over
And we looked at the dead objects.

Not still-lives any more but still-deaths.
Ruin comes so easily and reminds us
We too might have been destroyed;
I picked up a loved book but was dumb to tears.

And today I am numb still
Shocked to silence and lost
From such little tragedy.
Big ones build in the mind;
We are so near to paper
To nothingness
So, in the power of nature
I shall not light candles again for a long time.

The Luck

Be covetous of clouds. Stare as long as you like. They
cannot care.
Watch one star till it almost blinds you. Stand on a
narrow stair
And think how odd it is that here and now you are
Yourself and no-one else, but also a part
Of the world you sense everywhere.

Rabbit hiding, robin shivering, starling bold and sparrow,
All are part of you, you are never alone,
You are flesh, blood, veins, arteries, intricate bone
And you cannot last forever. You age every hour
But simply being and standing, even though sad,
Is a huge gift for there is an opposite of
All you think of and understand, all that you do not
know.
There is the swelling moon and there are your watching
eyes.
It is a bonus, a prize, an abundant gift
To be yourself with a mind that works in your head.

The First Music

What was the first music
After the chirping of birds, the barking of foxes,
After the hoot of owls, the mooing of cows,
The murmur of dawn birds, winds in the trees?
Did all these tell the first men they must make
Their own music? Mothers would lullaby
Their babies to sleep, warriors certainly shouted.
But what was the first music that was its own
Purpose, a pattern or phrasing, a quality
Of sound that came between silences and cast out
All other possible sounds? It must have been man
Singing in love and exultation, hearing
The high sweet song of blackbirds. When did he fashion
A harp or horn? O how much I would give
To hear that first and pristine music and know
That it changed the turning planet and visited stars.

Pigeons

Applaud the pigeon. Celebrate his ways.
In snow and frost and ice. In all bad weather,
Among stark cold and heat he always stays,
In this big freeze he and his buddies gather

With sharp eyes on a hand which may throw bread,
He has an instinct we have lost long since.
From far away he senses what we need
Our eyes or ears for. He's indeed a prince

And wears dull plumage like a uniform
Or robe that's fitting only for a king.
He balances on rooftops and keeps calm
While we are panicking at everything

We think we cannot do without. This bird
Shows up our pettiness, so let us feed
This one from whom a grumble's never heard,
Who trusts that we will satisfy his need.

Considering Magic

Don't think of magic as a conjuring trick
Or just as fortune-tellers reading hands
It is a secret which will sometimes break
Through ordinary days, and it depends

Upon right states of mind like good intent,
A love that's kind, a wisdom that is not
Pleased with itself. This sort of magic's meant
To cast a brilliance on dark trains of thought

And guide you through the mazes of the lost,
Lost love, lost people and lost animals.
For this, a sure, deep spell of care is cast

Which never lies and will not play you false.
It banishes the troubles of the past
And is the oldest way of casting spells.

Snake Charmer

The body writhes and rounds. The fingers feel
A circle, find a note. Up from the ground
Rears the caught serpent. It unwinds its coil
And dances to the sound

The player blows. His eyes address those eyes.
He is the choreographer who's made
The pattern of the dance, its length and size.
Danger is what is played.

In jeopardy, in thrall, the watchers can't
Help moving to the creature which they fear.
But they are safe as long as music's sent
Though that's not what they hear.

This is a rite but this is power also.
It happens now, yet enterprises such
As this take timid men to long ago
When the first reed's first touch

Haunted a jungle, hypnotised a snake.
This is no charming, this is courage when
At any moment faulty notes can break
Out anarchy again.

Spell of the Air

I am the impulse of all whispers, I
  Am the place for a rush of birds,
I am the whole intention of the sky
  And the place for coining words.

I am your life breathing in and out,
  I set your senses free,
I sort the truth from complicated doubt,
  I am necessity.

Emerging from a Cloud

Autumn

Fragile, notice that
As autumn starts, a light
Frost crisps up at night
And next day, for a while,
White covers path and lawn.
"Autumn is here, it is,"
Sings the stoical blackbird
But by noon pure gold is tossed
On everything. Leaves fall
As if they meant to rise.
Nothing of nature's lost.
The birth, the blight of things,
The bud, the stretching wings.

A Litany for Contrition

Dew on snowdrop
                weep for me
Rain in a rose
                cleanse my heart,
Bud of crocus
                candle me to
Contrition. Far stars
                shine from your great
Heights, and burn my faults away.
Half-moon emerging
                from a cloud
Strengthen my spirit.
                All spring flowers,
More each day,
                in this night now
Give me a scent of our sweet powers.
A shower of rain
                wash me clean,
Let my spirit glow
                for I have seen
The terrible depth
                of dark in me.
Christ, you alone
                can cure jealousy.

The Smell of Chrysanthemums

The chestnut leaves are toasted. Conkers spill
Upon the pavements. Gold is vying with
Yellow, ochre, brown. There is a feel
Of dyings and departures. Smoky breath
  Rises and I know how Winter comes
  When I can smell the rich chrysanthemums.

It is so poignant and it makes me mourn
For what? The going year? The sun's eclipse?
All these and more. I see the dead leaves burn
And everywhere the Summer lies in heaps.
  I close my eyes and feel how Winter comes
  With acrid incense of chrysanthemums.

I shall not go to school again and yet
There's an old sadness that disturbs me most.
The nights come early; every bold sunset
Tells me that Autumn soon will be a ghost,
  But I know best how Winter always comes
  In the wide scent of strong chrysanthemums.

A Christmas Sequence

II The Journey to Bethlehem

What is she thinking now
  As they ride through the cold
Toward Bethlehem? O how
  Can her God who is old

Or outside time at least
  Be growing in her womb?
This girl does not look blessed
  She fills so little room

Yet carries a new truth,
  A God whom she makes man
Will soon take his first breath
  And fit a lofty plan.

How can we not feel love
  To see such helplessness?
Our cold hearts start to move
  With an old gentleness,

Yet it is new also
  Since we are feeling for
A God who is to grow
  To manhood like the poor.

Listen, let Mary sing
  Her unborn child a cry
Such as all mothers bring
  To their first lullaby.

Meditation on the Nativity

All gods and goddesses, all looked up to
And argued with and threatened. All that fear
Which man shows to the very old and new –
All this, all these have gone. They disappear
In fables coming true,

In acts so simple that we are amazed –
A woman and a child. He trusts; she soothes.
Men see serenity and they are pleased.
Placating prophets talked but here are truths
All men have only praised

Before in dreams. Lost legends here are pressed
Not on to paper but in flesh and blood,
A promise kept. Her modesties divest
Our guilt of shame as she hands him her food
And he smiles on her breast.

Painters' perceptions, visionaries' long
Torments and silence, blossom here and speak.
Listen, our murmurs are a cradle-song,
Look, we are found who seldom dared to seek –
A maid, a child, God young.

Lazarus

It was the amazing white, it was the way he simply
Refused to answer our questions, it was the cold pale glance
Of death upon him, the smell of death that truly
Declared his rising to us. It was no chance
Happening, as a man may fill a silence
Between two heart-beats, seem to be dead and then
Astonish us with the closeness of his presence;
This man was dead, I say it again and again.
All of our sweating bodies moved towards him
And our minds moved too, hungry for finished faith.
He would not enter our world at once with words
That we might be tempted to twist or argue with:
Cold like a white root pressed in the bowels of earth
He looked, but also vulnerable – like birth.

In the bible Jesus raised Lazarus from the dead.

A Bird in the House

It was a yellow voice, a high, shrill treble in the nursery
White always and high, I remember it so,
White cupboard, off-white table, mugs, dolls' faces
And I was four or five. The garden could have been
Miles away. We were taken down to the green
Asparagus beds, the cut lawn, and the smell of it
Comes each summer after rain when white returns. Our
bird,
A canary called Peter, sang behind bars. The black and
white cat
Curled and snoozed by the fire and danger was far away.

Far away for us. Safety was life and only now do I know
That white walls and lit leaves knocking windows
Are a good prison but always you have
To escape, fly off from love not felt as love,
But our bird died in his yellow feathers. The quick
Cat caught him, tore him through bars when we were out
And I do not remember tears or sadness, I only
Remember the ritual, the warm yellow feathers we put
In a cardboard egg. What a sense of fitness. How far, I
know now,
Ritual goes back, egg to egg, birth to burial and we went
Down the garden softly, two in a small procession,
And the high clouds bent down, the sky pulled aside
Its blue curtains. Death was there or else
Where the wise cat had hidden. That day we buried our
bird
With a sense of fitness, not knowing death would be hard

Later, dark, without form or purpose.
After my first true grief I wept, was sad, was dark, but
today,
Clear of terror and agony,
The yellow bird sings in my mind and I say
That the child is callous but wise, knows the purpose of
play.
And the grief of ten years ago
Now has an ancient rite,
A walk down the garden carrying death in an egg
And the sky singing, the trees still waving farewell
When dying was nothing to know.

My Grandmother

She kept an antique shop – or it kept her.
Among Apostle spoons and Bristol glass,
The faded silks, the heavy furniture,
She watched her own reflection in the brass
Salvers and silver bowls, as if to prove
Polish was all, there was no need of love.

And I remember how I once refused
To go out with her, since I was afraid.
It was perhaps a wish not to be used
Like antique objects. Though she never said
That she was hurt, I still could feel the guilt
Of that refusal, guessing how she felt.

Later, too frail to keep a shop, she put
All her best things in one long narrow room.
The place smelt old, of things too long kept shut,
The smell of absences where shadows come
That can't be polished. There was nothing then
To give her own reflection back again.

And when she died I felt no grief at all,
Only the guilt of what I once refused.
I walked into her room among the tall
Sideboards and cupboards – things she never used
But needed; and no finger-marks were there,
Only the new dust falling through the air.

Persephone

For Spring and Summer she appeared and was
Blinded at first by light. To us she meant
Autumn and Winter were away because
For those two seasons she retreated, went

Back to the dark world, darker than our own.
When she arrived the petals opened to
Welcome her with their wreaths, twine round her throne.
Birds hatched their eggs and all things richly grew.

She went away quite silently one night.
The air was cold next day. From every tree
Leaves fell in dusty disarray to light
And burn the shadow of Persephone.

Persephone was the Greek goddess of the underworld, allowed to spend only part of each year on earth, thus symbolising regeneration.

Spell for Spring

I'll weave a spell and send it to
Friend after friend. It will bring you
Spring again with all its show
        Even if it is slow.

I'll cast a spell upon the land
And every field, and it will end
The winter's damage. You will see
        Blossom on every tree.

But there's another spell. It brings
Persephone and all the springs
That she has known.
            She casts a light.

We're dazzled by the sight.

Waking,
I Find Myself Alone

An Event

Legs in knee-socks,
Standing on the rough playground,
Suddenly thinking, "Why am I here?"

No one else seemed near you,
Though they had been, still were
Except for this awareness.

Long before adolescence
This happened, happened more than once.
Is this the onset

Of that long-travelling,
Never answered
Question, "Who am I?"

It could be.
The state does not last
But the memory does.

And soon the shouts surround you again.
You have a blue and a red marble in your hand.
It is your turn to roll one.

Holidays at Home

There was a family who, every year,
Would go abroad, sometimes to Italy,
Sometimes to France. The youngest did not dare
To say, "I much prefer to stay right here."

You see, abroad there were no slot-machines,
No bright pink rock with one name going through it,
No rain, no boarding-houses, no baked beans,
No landladies, and no familiar scenes.

And George, the youngest boy, so longed to say,
"I don't *like* Greece, I don't like all these views,
I don't like having fierce sun every day,
And, most of all, I just detest the way

The food is cooked – that garlic and that soup,
Those strings of pasta, and no cakes at all."
The family wondered why George seemed to droop
And looked just like a thin hen in a coop.

They never guessed why when they said, "Next year
We can't afford abroad, we'll stay right here",
George looked so pleased and soon began to dream
Of piers, pink rock, deep sand, and Devonshire cream.

The Circuses

On my first train at seven years old and the word
Circus running through my mind. The energetic
Clowns and sprightly horses and the elephants
Filled the ring, and a man in a top-hat
Conducted it all. How precise is the picture
Detailed from annuals and advertisements,
The primary colours dancing in my mind. London was all
The hush of dark around two rings. I had them
By heart and head. The train pulled in and the smoke
Seethed to the roof of Paddington. I noticed
Little. Even the waxworks were a prelude
For circling figures, rigorous patterns the ponies
Stepped to. We came to Oxford Circus and . . .
Why does the vision vanish? Why have I no record
Of total disappointment? What did I say when London
Shrank to high buses, screams of brakes and everywhere
Hoardings of grown-ups' dreams? So memory
Shields the future, dulls imagination
And no-one can tell me what I said or whether I cried
When the circle dwindled to traffic, the hope held nothing
inside.

The Dead Bird

(a poem I wrote when I was a child)

I held it in my hand
With its little hanging head.
It was soft and warm and whole,
But it was dead.

A Child in the Night

The child stares at the stars. He does not know
Their names. He does not care. Time halts for him
And he is standing on the earth's far rim
As all the sky surrenders its bright show.

He will not feel like this again until
He falls in love. He will not be possessed
By dispossession till he has caressed
A face and in its eyes seen stars stand still.

Given an Apple

He brought her an apple. She would not eat
And he was hurt until she said,
"I'm keeping it as a charm. It may
Grow small and wrinkled. I don't care.
I'll always think of you today.
Time is defeated for that hour
When you gave me an apple for
A love token, and more."

Friendship

Such love I cannot analyse;
It does not rest in lips or eyes,
Neither in kisses nor caress.
Partly, I know, it's gentleness

And understanding in one word
Or in brief letters. It's preserved
By trust and by respect and awe.
These are the words I'm feeling for.

Two people, yes, two lasting friends.
The giving comes, the taking ends.
There is no measure for such things.
For this all Nature slows and sings.

By the Sea

I have seen seas so still
That I could well believe
There was no sea at all.

But I have also seen
Great horses rearing up
And rushing down upon

The well-marked sand. Yes I
Know every mood and tense
Of tides. I was born by

The sea. I know its pulse
Since it still beats in me
From such great waterfalls.

Prisoner

Feel up the walls, waters ooze. The cold
Cranes down the spine. The wayward sky won't fit
A window, a square, but a square equates itself
With the eye in the brain, in the nervous system. All
Which flesh becomes without food and a little water.

I am tired. The planet curves, I cannot sleep.
How many moons have shone in how many shapes?
I am wistful in wisdom, honest in rich endearments,
Hollow perhaps, a channel for any whisper.
The long night takes my loneliness into its hands.

For my Sister

"I'm too old to play with you any more" –
The words mean laughter now. But did I care?
Your dozen years to my ten did no more
Than make me stubborn in my games. You were

A figure dwindling, lost among real babies,
Pushing prams, a little mother then
And I, when ill, would find you back again
Wheeling me round. Yes, you were everybody's

Nurse when they were broken, worn, afraid
But I was King of cross-roads, theatres, farms,
Vigilant, a lord of what I'd made,
Sometimes the rigid soldier bearing arms,
Sometimes a look-out on all thorough-fares.

"I'm too old . . ." You do not seem so now,
Seem yourself made perfect, and indeed
Matriarch, grandmother, careful wife,
Queen over sickness, and you come and go
Busy with all that makes a newborn life,
Fast and thorough. I'm the child still slow.

Old People

Why are people impatient when they are old?
Is it because they are tired of trying to make
Fast things move slowly?
I have seen their eyes flinch as they watch the lorries
Lurching and hurrying past.
I have also seen them twitch and move away
When a grandbaby cries.

They can go to the cinema cheaply,
They can do what they like all day.
Yet they shrink and shiver, looking like old, used dolls.
I do not think that I should like to be old.

For My Mother

I My Mother Dying Aged 87

You died as quietly as your spirit moved
All through my life. It was a shock to hear
Your shallow breathing and more hard to see
Your eyes closed fast. You did not wake for me
But even so I do not shed a tear.
Your spirit has flown free

Of that small shell of flesh. Grandchildren stood
Quietly by and it was they who gave
Most strength to us. They also loved you for
Your gentleness. You never made them fear
Anything. The memories you leave
Are happy times. You were

The one who gave me stamps and envelopes
And posted all my early poems. You had
Such faith in me. You could be firm and would
Curb tantrums, and would change an angry mood
With careful threats. I cannot feel too sad
Today for you were good

And that is what the kindly letters say.
Some are clumsy, some embarrass with
Lush piety but all will guide your ship
Upon a calm, bright ocean and we keep
Our eyes on it. It is too strong for death
And so we do not weep.

II Grief

I miss my mother today.
I went into a shop and saw the Mothering Sunday
Cards in bright array.
I always used to send her one and now
There is nothing to write or say.

Grief can strike you when
You least expect it. It's an emptiness
Easy to fill with pain.
My mother had no rage, was always kind.
When will she come again

And darken and haunt the large room of my mind?

When I Was Young

When I was young I wrote about the old.
Now I am old I write about the young.
The words are cautious for a worried world
And out of them I shape a tell-tale song.

I was irresponsible and wild
When I was young but now the young ones are
Thoughtful and anxious though their eyes are mild
Even when they speak to me of war.

They are prepared and do not blame the old
That many have to make the street their home.
I warm myself at their kind hearts. The cold
Shivers through me now long dark nights have come.

O but there is a joy that I would speak.
I have a dream and turn it to a song.
It is the only home that I can make.
Its doors are open to the careful young.

Our World Dreams Deep

Rhyme for Children

I am the seed that slept last night;
This morning I have grown upright.

Within my dream there was a king.
Now he is gone in the wide morning.

He had a queen, also a throne.
Waking, I find myself alone.

If I could have that dream again,
The seed should grow into a queen

And she should find at her right hand
A king to rule her heart and land:

And I would be the spring which burst
Beside their love and quenched their thirst.

Water Music

What I looked for was a place where water
Flowed continually. It could come
In rapids, over rocks in great falls and
Arrive at stillness far below. I watched
The hidden power. And then I went to rivers,
The source and mouth, the place where estuaries
Were the last, slow-moving waters and
The sea lay not far off continually
Making her music,
Loud gulls interrupting.
At first I only listened to her music,
Slow movements first, the held-back waves
With all their force to rear and roar and stretch
Over the waiting sand. Sea music is
What quiets my spirit. I would like my death
To come as rivers turn, as sea commands.
Let my last journey be to sounds of water.

Blackbird Singing

Out of that throat arise
  Such notes of poignant sound
That circle round the skies
  And never come to ground.

The bird has gone elsewhere
  But its melody echoes on
Through the transported air
  And it even gilds the sun.

Can any of us be
  So utterly outside our
Personal city
  Or the treading of the hour?

Never. O let it go
  On, this blackbird's song.
It has so much to show
  Our weakness. It is strong

But at least we recognise,
  Innocence, purity,
There is eloquence in the sky's
  Space and sweet energy.

Thunder and a Boy

(for T.)

That great bubble of silence, almost tangible quiet was shattered. There was no prelude, the huge chords
Broke and sounded timpani over the town, and then lightning, first darting, then strong bars
Taking hold of the sky, taking hold of us as we sank into primitive people,
Wondering at and frightened of the elements, forgetting so swiftly how naming had once seemed
To give them into our hands. Not any longer. We were powerless now completely.

But today we have risen with the rain and, though it is torrential, we believe at moments that we
Still have power over that. We are wrong. Those birds escaping through showers show us
They are more imperial than we are. We shift, talk, doze, look at papers,
Though one child is remembering how last night he stood with defiance

And joy at his window and shouted, "Do it again,
God, do it again!",
Can we say he was less wise than us? We cannot. He
acknowledged Zeus,
Thor, God the Father, and was prepared to cheer or
dispute with any of them.
This afternoon he watches the sky, praying the night will
show God's strength again
And he, without fear, feel those drums beating and
bursting through his defended, invisible mind.

Mary

I am afraid of people who move quickly,
Who jerk about and don't let you see their eyes.
Sometimes I think there are tigers lurking there.

At other times, I think these people move
Because they are not brave enough to be still.
If they stayed still,
If they stayed very still,
The tigers would be quiet.
Then one could feel their rough tongues licking,
And stroke their skins asleep.

The Secret Brother

Jack lived in the green-house
When I was six,
With glass and with tomato plants,
Not with slates and bricks.

I didn't have a brother,
Jack became mine.
Nobody could see him,
He never gave a sign.

Just beyond the rockery,
By the apple-tree,
Jack and his old mother lived,
Only for me.

With a tin telephone
Held beneath the sheet,
I would talk to Jack each night.
We would never meet.

Once my sister caught me,
Said, "He isn't there.
Down among the flower-pots
Cramm the gardener

Is the only person."
I said nothing, but
Let her go on talking.
Yet I moved Jack out.

He and his old mother
Did a midnight flit.
No one knew his number:
I had altered it.

Only I could see
The sagging washing-line
And my brother making
Our own secret sign.

Awake in the Siesta

Rumours of winds and dusty afternoons,
Others' siesta, I stay wideawake,
The only conscious one here. All cats sleep
Upon their shadows. Hot against the walls
Leaves and butterflies lick the crumbling stone.
Here was I, all by myself and happy,
Content in a country truly my first home.
So Tuscany about six years ago,
In a small town never sought out by tourists,
Nothing important, no mosaics and only
One small church not worth the sight-seer's inspection.
The view from my window was peerless, the shutters
  wide.
Everything I could possess but no possession.
I laid myself open to the atmosphere,
Dipped my hands in water.
                                        Tuscany
You are a sweetness in nostrils still,
A view I'd never trade, and, every morning
The promising haze and the emerging hills.

Song of Love and Peace

Love, be a bird to me,
  Lullaby me, wake
Me to the dawn and the
  Voices of day-break.

Love, I will sing you to
  A sleep dividing us.
I'll wake you to the true
  Dawn, day's impetus.

Love, let us wind round
  Each other silence, peace
Deeper than silence. Sound
  Is far away from us.

Morning we'll enter with
  The birds. When shall we speak?
Not till the first bird's breath
  Sings us wide awake.

Lullaby

Sleep, my baby, the night is coming soon.
Sleep, my baby, the day has broken down.

Sleep now: let silence come, let the shadows form
A castle of strength for you, a fortress of calm.

You are so small, sleep will come with ease.
Hush now, be still now, join the silences.

Night Moment

One cedar tree, one oak, one sycamore
  Turn in a little sigh
Of wind. This is the day's evasive hour,
  For now the quick-change sky

Is restive, paling, sinking, letting go,
  Her anchor pulls away.
Moment by moment all the trees will show
  A branch of stars to stay

Until the morning. Under those stars sleep
  Or at least lie peacefully.
All bird-calls have just stopped. Our world dreams deep
  And for ten hours is free.

Index of First Lines

Sources

The poems in this selection first appeared in the following collections.

Previously unpublished: Pigeons (not to be confused with poem of same title from *Recoveries*), Clouds, Remember, Spell of the Air, The Luck

Casting a Spell (anthology) ed. Angela Huth (Orchard 1991): Considering Magic, Casting a Spell

The Secret Brother (Macmillan 1966): The Secret Brother, Holidays at Home, A Sort of Chinese Poem, The Ark, Tiffany: a Burmese Kitten, Rhyme for Children, Old People, Mary, The Dead Bird, Lullaby

Song for A Birth or A Death (André Deutsch 1961): My Grandmother, Lazarus, In Praise of Creation

The Animals' Arrival (Macmillan 1969): Fire, The Animals' Arrival

Relationships (Macmillan 1972): Friendship

Growing Points (Carcanet 1975): Beech, Thunder and a Boy, Bird Study, Meditation on the Nativity, Persephone, Snake Charmer, Prisoner, Losing and Finding, An Event, An Attempt to Charm Sleep

Consequently, I Rejoice (Carcanet 1977): Hatching, A Child in the Night

After the Ark (OUP 1978): All 29 poems

Moments of Grace (Carcanet 1979): Goldfinch, Night Moment

Celebrations and Elegies (Carcanet 1982): Autumn, Sparrow, Blackbird Singing, Given an Apple, Song of Love and Peace

Extending the Territory (Carcanet 1985): A Bird in the House, For My Sister, The Circuses, A Classroom, Ballad of War, Awake in the Siesta, A Performance of Henry V at Stratford-upon-Avon, Water Music, By the Sea, Spell for Spring

Tributes (Carcanet 1989): Beginning

Time and Seasons (Carcanet 1992): For My Mother, The Smell of Chrysanthemums, A Christmas Sequence: II The Journey to Bethlehem, A Litany for Contrition, Think Of, Star-Gazing, When I Was Young

Familiar Spirits (Carcanet 1994): The First Music